A Difficult Problem

Anna Katharine Green

Pharos Books

HB ISBN: 978-93-71417-31-0
ISBN: 978-93-59832-01-2
eISBN: 978-93-59830-11-7

Publisher: Pharos Books (P) Ltd.
Plot No.-63, 1st Floor, Main Mother Dairy Road
Pandav Nagar, East Delhi-110092
Phone: 011-40395855, +4049916623
WhatsApp: +91 9319228272
E-mail: bookspharos@gmail.com
Website: www.pharosbooks.in
Edition: 2025

Printed By: Sushma Book Binding House, Okhla Industrial Area, Phase II, New Delhi-110020

A DIFFICULT PROBLEM
Anna Katharine Green

A DIFFICULT PROBLEM

A DIFFICULT PROBLEM

I.

"A LADY to see you, sir."

I looked up and was at once impressed by the grace and beauty of the person thus introduced to me.

"Is there anything I can do to serve you?" I asked, rising.

She cast me a child-like look full of trust and candor as she seated herself in the chair I pointed out to her.

"I believe so, I hope so," she earnestly assured me. "I—I am in great trouble. I have just lost my husband—but it is not that. It is the slip of paper I found on my dresser, and which—which—"

She was trembling violently and her words were fast becoming incoherent. I calmed her and asked her to relate her story just as it had happened; and after a few minutes of silent struggle she succeeded in collecting herself sufficiently to respond with some degree of connection and self-possession.

"I have been married six months. My name is Lucy Holmes. For the last few weeks my husband and myself have been living in an apartment house on Fifty-ninth Street, and as we had not a care in the world, we were very happy till Mr. Holmes was called away on business to Philadelphia. This was two weeks ago. Five days later I received an affectionate letter from him, in which he promised to come back the next day; and the news so delighted me that I accepted an invitation to the theater from some intimate friends of ours. The next morning I naturally felt fatigued and rose late; but I was very cheerful, for I expected my husband at noon. And now comes the perplexing mystery. In the course of dressing myself I stepped to my bureau, and seeing a small newspaper-slip attached to the cushion by a pin, I drew it off and read it. It was a death notice, and my hair rose and my limbs failed me as I took in its fatal and incredible words.

"'Died this day at the Colonnade, James Forsythe De Witt Holmes. New York papers please copy.'

"James Forsythe De Witt Holmes was my husband, and his last letter, which was at that very moment lying beside the cushion, had been dated from the Colonnade. Was I dreaming or under the spell of some frightful hallucination which led me to misread the name on the slip of paper before me? I could not determine. My head, throat and chest seemed bound about with iron, so that I could neither speak nor breathe with freedom, and, suffering thus, I stood staring at this demoniacal bit of paper which in an instant had brought the shadow of death upon my happy life. Nor was I at all relieved when a little later I flew with the notice into a neighbor's apartment, and praying her to read it for me, found that my eyes had not deceived me and that the name was indeed my husband's and the notice one of death.

"Not from my own mind but from hers came the first suggestion of comfort.

"'It cannot be your husband who is meant,' said she; 'but some one of the same name. Your husband wrote to you yesterday, and this person must have been dead at least two days for the printed notice of his decease to have reached New York. Some one has remarked the striking similarity of names, and wishing to startle you, cut the slip out and pinned it on your cushion.'

"I certainly knew of no one inconsiderate enough to do this, but the explanation was so plausible, I at once embraced it and sobbed aloud in my relief. But in the midst of my rejoicing I heard the bell ring in my apartment, and running thither, encountered a telegraph boy holding in his outstretched hand the yellow envelope which so often bespeaks death or disaster. The sight took my breath away. Summoning my maid, whom I saw hastening towards me from an inner room, I begged her to open the telegram for me. Sir, I saw in her face, before she had read the first line, a confirmation of my very worst fears. My husband was—"

The young widow, choked with her emotions, paused, recovered herself for the second time, and then went on.

"I had better show you the telegram." Taking it from her pocket-book, she held it towards me. I read it at a glance. It was short, simple and direct.

"Come at once. Your husband found dead in his room this morning. Doctors say heart disease. Please telegraph."

"You see it says this morning," she explained, placing her delicate finger on the word she so eagerly quoted. "That means a week ago Wednesday, the same day on which the printed slip recording his death was found on my cushion. Do you not see something very strange in this?"

I did; but, before I ventured to express myself on this subject, I desired her to tell me what she had learned in her visit to Philadelphia.

Her answer was simple and straightforward.

"But little more than you find in this telegram. He died in his room. He was found lying on the floor near the bell button, which he had evidently risen to touch. One hand was clenched on his chest, but his face wore a peaceful look as if death had come too suddenly to cause him much suffering. His bed was undisturbed; he had died before retiring, possibly in the act of packing his trunk, for it was found nearly ready for the expressman. Indeed, there was every evidence of his intention to leave on an early morning train. He had even desired to be awakened at six o'clock; and it was his failure to respond to the summons of the bell-boy, which led to so early a discovery of his death. He had never complained of any distress in breathing, and we had always considered him a perfectly healthy man; but there was no reason for assigning any other cause than heart-failure to his sudden death, and so the burial certificate was made out to that effect, and I was allowed to bring him home and bury him in our vault at Wood-lawn. But—" and here her earnestness dried up the tears which had been flowing freely during this recital of her husband's lonely death and sad burial,—"do you not think an investigation should be made into a death preceded by a false obituary notice? For I found when I was in Philadelphia that no paragraph such as I had found pinned to my cushion had been inserted in any paper there, nor had any other man of the same name ever registered at the Colonnade, much less died there."

"Have you this notice with you?" I asked.

She immediately produced it, and while I was glancing it over remarked:

"Some persons would give a superstitious explanation to the whole matter; think I had received a supernatural warning and been satisfied with what they would call a spiritual manifestation. But I have not a bit of such folly in my composition. Living hands set up the type and printed the words which gave me so deathly a shock; and hands, with a real purpose in them, cut it from the paper and pinned it to my cushion for me to see when I woke on that fatal morning. But whose hands? That is what I want you to discover."

I had caught the fever of her suspicions long before this and now felt justified in showing my interest.

"First, let me ask," said I, "who has access to your rooms besides your maid?"

"No one; absolutely no one."

"And what of her?"

"She is innocence itself. She is no common housemaid, but a girl my mother brought up, who for love of me consents to do such work in the household as my simple needs require."

"I should like to see her."

"There is no objection to your doing so; but you will gain nothing by it. I have already talked the subject over with her a dozen times and she is as much puzzled by it as I am myself. She says she cannot see how any one could have found an entrance to my room during my sleep, as the doors were all locked. Yet, as she very naturally observes, some one must have done so, for she was in my bedroom herself just before I returned from the theater, and can swear, if necessary, that no such slip of paper was to be seen on my cushion, at that time, for her duties led her directly to my bureau and kept her there for full five minutes."

"And you believed her?" I suggested.

"Implicitly."

"In what direction, then, do your suspicions turn?"

"Alas! in no direction. That is the trouble. I don't know whom to mistrust. It was because I was told that you had the credit of seeing light where others can see nothing but darkness, that I have sought your aid in this emergency. For the uncertainty surrounding this matter is killing me and will make my sorrow quite unendurable if I cannot obtain relief from it."

"I do not wonder," I began, struck by the note of truth in her tones. "And I shall certainly do what I can for you. But before we go any further, let us examine this scrap of newspaper and see what we can make out of it."

I had already noted two or three points in connection with it, to which I now proceeded to direct her attention.

"Have you compared this notice," I pursued, "with such others as you find every day in the papers?"

"No," was her eager answer. "Is it not like them all—"

"Read," was my quiet interruption. "'On this day at the Colonnade—' On what day? The date is usually given in all the **bona-fide** notices I have seen."

"Is it?" she asked, her eyes moist with un-shed tears, opening widely in her astonishment.

"Look in the papers on your return home and see. Then the print. Observe that the type is identical on both sides of this make-believe clipping, while in fact there is always a perceptible difference between that used in the obituary column and that to be found in the columns devoted to other matter. Notice also," I continued, holding up the scrap of paper between her and the light, "that the alignment on one side is not exactly parallel with that on the other; a discrepancy which would not exist if both sides had been printed on a newspaper press. These facts lead me to conclude, first, that the effort to match the type exactly was the mistake of a man who tries to do too much; and secondly, that one of the sides at least, presumably that containing the obituary notice, was printed on a hand-press, on the blank side of a piece of galley proof picked up in some newspaper office."

"Let me see." And stretching out her hand with the utmost eagerness, she took the slip and turned it over. Instantly a change took place in her countenance. She sank back in her seat and a blush of manifest confusion suffused her cheeks. "Oh!" she exclaimed, "what will you think of me! I brought this scrap of print into the house **myself** and it was **I** who pinned it on the cushion with my own hands! I remember it now. The sight of those words recalls the whole occurrence."

"Then there is one mystery less for us to solve," I remarked, somewhat dryly.

"Do you think so," she protested, with a deprecatory look. "For me the mystery deepens, and becomes every minute more serious. It is true that I brought this scrap of newspaper into the house, and that it had, then as now, the notice of my husband's death upon it, but the time of my bringing it in was Tuesday night, and he was not found dead till Wednesday morning."

"A discrepancy worth noting," I remarked.

"Involving a mystery of some importance," she concluded.

I agreed to that.

"And since we have discovered how the slip came into your room, we can now proceed to the clearing up of this mystery," I observed. "You can, of course, inform me where you procured this clipping which you say you brought into the house?"

"Yes. You may think it strange, but when I alighted from the carriage that night, a man on the sidewalk put this tiny scrap of paper into my hand. It was done so mechanically that it made no more impression on my mind than the thrusting of an advertisement upon me. Indeed, I supposed it was an advertisement, and I only wonder that I retained it in my hand at all. But that I did do so, and that, in a moment of abstraction I went so far as to pin it to my cushion, is evident from the fact that a vague memory remains in my mind of having read this recipe which you see printed on the reverse side of the paper."

"It was the recipe, then, and not the obituary notice which attracted your attention the night before?"

"Probably, but in pinning it to the cushion, it was the obituary notice that chanced to come uppermost. Oh, why should I not have remembered this till now! Can you understand my forgetting a matter of so much importance?"

"Yes," I allowed, after a momentary consideration of her ingenuous countenance. "The words you read in the morning were so startling that they disconnected themselves from those you had carelessly glanced at the night before."

"That is it," she replied; "and since then I have had eyes for the one side only. How could I think of the other? But who could have printed this thing and who was the man who put it into my hand? He looked like a beggar but—Oh!" she suddenly exclaimed, her cheeks flushing scarlet and her eyes flashing with a feverish, almost alarming, glitter.

"What is it now?" I asked. "Another recollection?"

"Yes." She spoke so low I could hardly hear her. "He coughed and—"

"And what?" I encouragingly suggested, seeing that she was under some new and overwhelming emotion.

"That cough had a familiar sound, now that I think of it. It was like that of a friend who—But no, no; I will not wrong him by any false surmises. He would stoop to much, but not to that; yet—"

The flush on her cheeks had died away, but the two vivid spots which remained showed the depth of her excitement.

"Do you think," she suddenly asked, "that a man out of revenge might plan to frighten me by a false notice of my husband's death, and that God to punish him, made the notice a prophecy?"

"I think a man influenced by the spirit of revenge might do almost anything," I answered, purposely ignoring the latter part of her question.

"But I always considered him a good man. At least I never looked upon him as a wicked one. Every other beggar we meet has a cough; and yet," she added after a moment's pause, "if it was not he who gave me this mortal shock, who was it? He is the only person in the world I ever wronged."

"Had you not better tell me his name?" I suggested.

"No, I am in too great doubt. I should hate to do him a second injury."

"You cannot injure him if he is innocent. My methods are very safe."

"If I could forget his cough! but it had that peculiar catch in it that I remembered so well in the cough of John Graham. I did not pay any especial heed to it at the time. Old days and old troubles were far enough from my thoughts; but now that my suspicions are raised, that low, choking sound comes back to me in a strangely persistent way, and I seem to see a well-remembered form in the stooping figure of this beggar. Oh, I hope the good God will forgive me if I attribute to this disappointed man a wickedness he never committed."

"Who is John Graham?" I urged, "and what was the nature of the wrong you did him?"

She rose, cast me one appealing glance, and perceiving that I meant to have her whole story, turned towards the fire and stood warming her feet before the hearth, with her face turned away from my gaze.

"I was once engaged to marry him," she began. "Not because I loved him, but because we were very poor—I mean my mother and myself—and he had a home and seemed both good and generous. The day came when we were to be married—this was in the West, way out in Kansas—and I was even dressed for the wedding, when a letter came from my uncle here, a rich uncle, very rich, who had never had anything to do with my mother since her marriage, and in it he promised me fortune and everything else desirable in life if I would come to him, unencumbered by any foolish ties. Think of it! And I within half an hour of marriage with a man I had never loved and now suddenly hated. The temptation was overwhelming, and heartless as my conduct may appear to you, I succumbed to it. Telling my lover that I had changed my mind, I dismissed the minister when he came, and announced my intention of proceeding East as soon as possible. Mr. Graham was simply paralyzed by his disappointment, and during the few days which intervened before my departure, I was haunted by his face, which was like that of a man who had died from some overwhelming shock. But when I was once free of the town, especially after I arrived in New York, I forgot alike his misery and himself. Everything I saw was so beautiful! Life was so full of charm, and my uncle so delighted with me and everything I did! Then there was James Holmes, and after I had seen him—But I cannot talk of that. We loved each other, and under the surprise of this new delight how could I be expected to remember the man I had left behind me in that barren region in which I had spent my youth? But he did not forget the misery I had caused him. He followed me to New York: and on the morning I was married found his way into the house, and mixing with the wedding guests, suddenly appeared before me just as I was receiving the congratulations of my friends. At sight of him I experienced all the terror he had calculated upon causing, but remembering at whose side I stood, I managed to hide my confusion under an aspect of apparent haughtiness. This irritated John Graham. Flushing with anger, and ignoring my imploring look, he cried peremptorily, 'Present me to your husband!' and I felt forced to present him. But his name produced no effect upon Mr. Holmes. I had never told him of my early experience with this man, and John Graham, perceiving this, cast me a bitter glance of disdain and passed on, muttering between his teeth, 'False to me and false to him! Your punishment be upon you!' and I felt as if I had been cursed."

She stopped here, moved by emotions readily to be understood. Then with quick impetuosity she caught up the thread of her story and went on.

"That was six months ago; and again I forgot. My mother died and my husband soon absorbed my every thought. How could I dream that this man, who was little more than a memory to me and scarcely that, was secretly planning mischief against me? Yet this scrap about which we have talked so much may have been the work of his hands; and even my husband's death—"

She did not finish, but her face, which was turned towards me, spoke volumes.

"Your husband's death shall be inquired into," I assured her. And she, exhausted by the excitement of her discoveries, asked that she might be excused from further discussion of the subject at that time.

As I had no wish, myself, to enter any more fully into the matter just then, I readily acceded to her request, and the pretty widow left me.

II.

Obviously the first fact to be settled was whether Mr. Holmes had died from purely natural causes. I accordingly busied myself the next few days with this question, and was fortunate enough to so interest the proper authorities that an order was issued for the exhumation and examination of the body.

The result was disappointing. No traces of poison were to be, found in the stomach nor was there to be seen on the body any mark of violence, with the exception of a minute prick upon one of his thumbs.

This speck was so small that it escaped every eye but my own.

The authorities assuring the widow that the doctor's certificate given her in Philadelphia was correct, he was again interred. But I was not satisfied; neither do I think she was. I was confident that his death was not a natural one, and entered upon one of those secret and prolonged investigations which have constituted the pleasure of my life for so many years. First, I visited the Colonnade in Philadelphia, and being allowed to see the room in which Mr. Holmes died, went through it carefully. As it had not been used since that time I had some hopes of coming upon a clue.

But it was a vain hope and the only result of my journey to this place was the assurance I received that the gentleman had spent the entire evening preceding his death, in his own room, where he had been brought several letters and one small package, the latter coming by mail. With this one point gained—if it was a point—I went back to New York.

Calling on Mrs. Holmes, I asked her if, while her husband was away she had sent him anything besides letters, and upon her replying to the contrary, requested to know if in her visit to Philadelphia she had noted among her husband's effects anything that was new or unfamiliar to her, "For he received a package while there," I explained, "and though its contents may have been perfectly harmless, it is just as well for us to be assured of this, before going any further."

"Oh, you think, then, he was really the victim of some secret violence."

"We have no proof of it," I said. "On the contrary, we are assured that he died from natural causes. But the incident of the newspaper slip outweighs, in my mind, the doctor's conclusions, and until the mystery surrounding that obituary notice has been satisfactorily explained by its author, I shall hold to the theory that your husband has been made away with in some strange and seemingly unaccountable manner, which it is our duty to bring to light."

"You are right! You are right! Oh, John Graham!"

She was so carried away by this plain expression of my belief that she forgot the question I had put to her.

"You have not told whether or not you found anything among your husband's effects that can explain this mystery," I suggested.

She at once became attentive.

"Nothing," said she: "his trunks were already packed and his bag nearly so. There were a few things lying about the room which were put into the latter, but I saw nothing but what was familiar to me among them; at least, I think not; perhaps we had better look through his trunk and see. I have not had the heart to open it since I came back."

As this was exactly what I wished, I said as much, and she led me into a small room, against the wall of which stood a trunk with a traveling-bag on top of it. Opening the latter, she spread the contents out on the trunk.

"I know all these things," she sadly murmured, the tears welling in her eyes.

"This?" I inquired, lifting up a bit of coiled wire with two or three little rings dangling from it.

"No; why, what is that?"

"It looks like a puzzle of some kind."

"Then it is of no consequence. My husband was forever amusing himself over some such contrivance. All his friends knew how well he liked these toys and frequently sent them to him. This one evidently reached him in Philadelphia."

Meanwhile I was eying the bit of wire curiously. It was undoubtedly a puzzle, but it had appendages to it that I did not understand.

"It is more than ordinarily complicated," I observed, moving the rings up and down in a vain endeavor to work them off.

"The better he would like it," said she.

I kept on working with the rings. Suddenly I gave a painful start. A little prong in the handle of the toy had started out and pricked me.

"You had better not handle it," said I, and laid it down. But the next minute I took it up again and put it in my pocket. The prick made by this treacherous bit of mechanism was in or near the same place on my thumb as the one I had noticed on the hand of the deceased Mr. Holmes.

There was a fire in the room, and before proceeding further, I cauterized that prick with the end of a red-hot poker. Then I made my adieux to Mrs. Holmes and went immediately to a chemist friend of mine.

"Test the end of this bit of steel for me," said I. "I have reason to believe it carries with it a deadly poison."

He took the toy, promised to subject it to every test possible and let me know the result. Then I went home. I felt ill, or imagined that I did, which under the circumstances was almost as bad.

Next day, however, I was quite well, with the exception of a certain inconvenience in my thumb. But not till the following week did I receive the chemist's report. It overthrew my whole theory. He had found nothing, and returned me the bit of steel.

But I was not convinced.

"I will hunt up this John Graham," thought I, "and study him."

But this was not so easy a task as it may appear. As Mrs. Holmes possessed no clue to the whereabouts of her quondam lover, I had nothing to aid me in my search for him, save her rather vague description of his personal appearance and the fact that he was constantly interrupted in speaking by a low, choking cough. However, my natural perseverance carried me through. After seeing and interviewing a dozen John Grahams without result, I at last lit upon a man of that name who presented a figure of such vivid unrest and showed such desperate hatred of his fellows, that I began to entertain hopes of his being the person I was in search of. But determined to be sure of this before proceeding further, I confided my suspicions to Mrs. Holmes, and induced her to accompany me down to a certain spot on the "Elevated" from which I had more than once seen this man go by to his usual lounging place in Printing-house Square.

She showed great courage in doing this, for she had such a dread of him that she was in a state of nervous excitement from the moment she left her house, feeling sure that she would attract his attention and thus risk a disagreeable encounter. But she might have spared herself these fears. He did not even glance up in passing us, and it was mainly by his walk she recognized him. But she did recognize him; and this nerved me at once to set about the formidable task of fixing upon him a crime which was not even admitted as a fact by the authorities.

He was a man-about-town, living, to all appearance, by his wits. He was to be seen mostly in the downtown portions of the city, standing for hours in front of some newspaper office, gnawing at his finger-ends, and staring at the passers-by with a hungry look that alarmed the timid and provoked alms from the benevolent. Needless to say that he rejected the latter expression of sympathy, with angry contempt.

His face was long and pallid, his cheek-bones high and his mouth bitter and resolute in expression. He wore neither beard nor mustache, but made up for their lack by an abundance of light brown hair, which hung very nearly to his shoulders. He stooped in standing, but as soon as he moved, showed decision and a certain sort of pride which caused him to hold his head high and his body more than usually erect. With all these good points his appearance was decidedly sinister, and I did not wonder that Mrs. Holmes feared him.

My next move was to accost him. Pausing before the doorway in which he stood, I addressed him some trivial question. He answered me with sufficient politeness, but with a grudging attention which betrayed the hold which his own thoughts had upon him. He coughed while speaking and his eye, which for a moment rested on mine, produced upon me an impression for which I was hardly prepared, great as was my prejudice against him. There was such an icy composure in it; the composure of an envenomed nature conscious of its superiority to all surprise. As I lingered to study him more closely, the many dangerous qualities of the man became more and more apparent to me; and convinced that to proceed further without deep and careful thought, would be to court failure where triumph would set me up for life, I gave up all present attempt at enlisting him in conversation, and went my way in an inquiring and serious mood.

In fact, my position was a peculiar one, and the problem I had set for myself one of unusual difficulty. Only by means of some extraordinary device such as is seldom resorted to by the police of this or any other nation, could I hope to arrive at the secret of this man's conduct, and triumph in a matter which to all appearance was beyond human penetration.

But what device? I knew of none, nor through two days and nights of strenuous thought did I receive the least light on the subject. Indeed, my mind seemed to grow more and more confused the more I urged it into action. I failed to get inspiration indoors or out; and feeling my health suffer from the constant irritation of my recurring disappointment, I resolved to take a day off and carry myself and my perplexities into the country.

I did so. Governed by an impulse which I did not then understand, I went to a small town in New Jersey and entered the first house on which I saw the sign "Room to Let." The result was most fortunate. No sooner had I crossed the threshold of the neat and homely apartment thrown open to my use, than it recalled a room in which I had slept two years before and in which I had read a little book I was only too glad to remember at this moment. Indeed, it seemed as if a veritable inspiration had come to me through this recollection, for though the tale to which I allude was a simple child's story written for moral purposes, it contained an idea which promised to be invaluable to me at this juncture. Indeed, by means of it, I believed myself to have solved the problem that was puzzling me, and relieved beyond expression, I paid for the night's lodging I had now determined to forego, and returned immediately to New York, having spent just fifteen minutes in the town where I had received this happy inspiration.

My first step on entering the city was to order a dozen steel coils made similar to the one which I still believed answerable for James Holmes' death. My next to learn as far as possible all of John Graham's haunts and habits. At a week's end I had the springs and knew almost as well as he did himself where he was likely to be found at all times of the day and night. I immediately acted upon this knowledge. Assuming a slight disguise, I repeated my former stroll through Printing-house Square, looking into each doorway as I passed. John Graham was in one of them, staring in his old way at the passing crowd, but evidently seeing nothing but the images formed by his own disordered brain. A manuscript-roll stuck out of his breast-pocket, and from the way his nervous fingers fumbled with it, I began to understand the restless glitter of his eyes, which were as full of wretchedness as any eyes I have ever seen.

Entering the doorway where he stood, I dropped at his feet one of the small steel coils with which I was provided. He did not see it. Stopping near him I directed his attention to it by saying:

"Pardon me, but did I not see something drop out of your hand?"

He started, glanced at the seeming inoffensive toy at which I pointed, and altered so suddenly and so vividly that it became instantly apparent that the surprise I had planned for him was fully as keen and searching a one as I had anticipated. Recoiling sharply, he gave me a quick look, then glanced down again at his feet as if half expecting to find the object vanished which had startled him. But, perceiving it still lying there, he crushed it viciously with his heel, and uttering some incoherent words, dashed impetuously from the building.

Confident that he would regret this hasty impulse and return, I withdrew a few steps and waited. And sure enough, in less than five minutes he came slinking back. Picking up the coil with more than one sly look about, he examined it closely. Suddenly he gave a sharp cry and went staggering out. Had he discovered that the seeming puzzle possessed the same invisible spring which had made the one handled by James Holmes so dangerous?

Certain as to the place he would be found in next, I made a short cut to an obscure little saloon in Nassau Street, where I took up my stand in a spot convenient for seeing without being seen. In ten minutes he was standing at the bar asking for a drink.

"Whiskey!" he cried, "straight."

It was given him; but as he set the empty glass down on the counter, he saw lying before him another of the steel springs, and was so confounded by the sight that the proprietor, who had put it there at my instigation, thrust out his hand toward him as if half afraid he would fall.

"Where did that—that **thing** come from?" stammered John Graham, ignoring the other's gesture and pointing with a trembling hand at the seemingly insignificant bit of wire between them.

"Didn't it drop from your coat-pocket?" inquired the proprietor. "It wasn't lying here before you came in."

With a horrible oath the unhappy man turned and fled from the place. I lost sight of him after that for three hours, then I suddenly came upon him again. He was walking up town with a set purpose in his face that made him look more dangerous than ever. Of course I followed him, expecting him to turn towards Fifty-ninth Street, but at the corner of Madison Avenue and Forty-seventh Street he changed his mind and dashed toward Third Avenue. At Park Avenue he faltered and again turned north, walking for several blocks as if the fiends were behind him. I began to think that he was but attempting to walk off his excitement, when, at a sudden rushing sound in the cut beside us, he stopped and trembled. An express train was shooting by. As it disappeared in the tunnel beyond, he looked about him with a blanched face and wandering eye; but his glance did not turn my way, or if it did, he failed to attach any meaning to my near presence.

He began to move on again and this time towards the bridge spanning the cut. I followed him very closely. In the center of it he paused and looked down at the track beneath him. Another train was approaching. As it came near he trembled from head to foot, and catching at the railing against which he leaned, was about to make a quick move forward when a puff of smoke arose from below and sent him staggering backward, gasping with a terror I could hardly understand till I saw that the smoke had taken the form of a spiral and was sailing away before him in what to his disordered imagination must have looked like a gigantic image of the coil with which twice before on this day he had found himself confronted.

It may have been chance and it may have been providence; but whichever it was it saved him. He could not face that semblance of his haunting thought; and turning away he cowered down on the neighboring curbstone, where he sat for several minutes, with his head buried in his hands; when he rose again he was his own daring and sinister self. Knowing that he was now too much master of his faculties to ignore me any longer, I walked quickly away and left him. I knew where he would be at six o'clock and had already engaged a table at the same restaurant. It was seven, however, before he put in an appearance, and by this time he was looking more composed. There was a reckless air about him, however, which was perhaps only noticeable to me; for none of the habitues of this especial restaurant were entirely without it; wild eyes and unkempt hair being in the majority.

I let him eat. The dinner he ordered was simple and I had not the heart to interrupt his enjoyment of it.

But when he had finished; and came to pay, then I allowed the shock to come. Under the bill which the waiter laid at the side of his plate was the inevitable steel coil; and it produced even more than its usual effect. I own I felt sorry for him.

He did not dash from the place, however, as he had from the liquor-saloon. A spirit of resistance had seized him and he demanded to know where this object of his fear had come from. No one could tell him (or would). Whereupon he began to rave and would certainly have done himself or somebody else an injury if he had not been calmed by a man almost as wild-looking as himself. Paying his bill, but vowing he would never enter the place again, he went out, clay-white, but with the swaggering air of a man who had just asserted himself.

He drooped, however, as soon as he reached the street, and I had no difficulty in following him to a certain gambling den where he gained three dollars and lost five. From there he went to his lodgings in West Tenth Street.

I did not follow him in. He had passed through many deep and wearing emotions since noon, and I had not the heart to add another to them.

But late the next day I returned to this house and rang the bell. It was already dusk, but there was light enough for me to notice the unrepaired condition of the iron railings on either side of the old stone stoop and to compare this abode of decayed grandeur with the spacious and elegant apartment in which pretty Mrs. Holmes mourned the loss of her young husband. Had any such comparison ever been made by the unhappy John Graham, as he hurried up these decayed steps into the dismal halls beyond?

In answer to my summons there came to the door a young woman to whom I had but to intimate my wish to see Mr. Graham for her to let me in with the short announcement:

"Top floor, back room! Door open, he's out; door shut, he's in."

As an open door meant liberty to enter, I lost no time in following the direction of her pointing finger, and presently found myself in a low attic chamber overlooking an acre of roofs. A fire had been lighted in the open grate, and the flickering red beams danced on ceiling and walls with a cheeriness greatly in contrast to the nature of the business which had led me there. As they also served to light the room I proceeded to make myself at home; and drawing up a chair, sat down at the fireplace in such a way as to conceal myself from any one entering the door.

In less than half an hour he came in.

He was in a state of high emotion. His face was flushed and his eyes burning. Stepping rapidly forward, he flung his hat on the table in the middle of the room, with a curse that was half cry and half groan. Then he stood silent and I had an opportunity of noting how haggard he had grown in the short time which had elapsed since I had seen him last. But the interval of his inaction was short, and in a moment he flung up his arms with a loud "Curse her!" that rang through the narrow room and betrayed the source of his present frenzy. Then he again stood still, grating his teeth and working his hands in a way terribly suggestive of the murderer's instinct. But not for long. He saw something that attracted his attention on the table, a something upon which my eyes had long before been fixed, and starting forward with a fresh and quite different display of emotion, he caught up what looked like a roll of manuscript and began to tear it open.

"Back again! Always back!" wailed from his lips; and he gave the roll a toss that sent from its midst a small object which he no sooner saw than he became speechless and reeled back. It was another of the steel coils.

"Good God!" fell at last from his stiff and working lips. "Am I mad or has the devil joined in the pursuit against me? I cannot eat, I cannot drink, but this diabolical spring starts up before me. It is here, there, everywhere. The visible sign of my guilt; the—the——" He had stumbled back upon my chair, and turning, saw me.

I was on my feet at once, and noting that he was dazed by the shock of my presence, I slid quietly between him and the door.

The movement roused him. Turning upon me with a sarcastic smile in which was concentrated the bitterness of years, he briefly said:

"So, I am caught! Well, there has to be an end to men as well as to things, and I am ready for mine. She turned me away from her door to-day, and after the hell of that moment I don't much fear any other."

"You had better not talk," I admonished him. "All that falls from you now will only tell against you on your trial."

He broke into a harsh laugh. "And do you think I care for that? That having been driven by a woman's perfidy into crime I am going to bridle my tongue and keep down the words which are my only safeguard from insanity? No, no; while my miserable breath lasts I will curse her, and if the halter is to cut short my words, it shall be with her name blistering my lips."

I attempted to speak, but he would not give me the opportunity. The passion of weeks had found vent and he rushed on recklessly.

"I went to her house to-day. I wanted to see her in her widow's weeds; I wanted to see her eyes red with weeping over a grief which owed its bitterness to me. But she would not grant me an admittance. She had me thrust from her door, and I shall never know how deeply the iron has sunk into her soul. But—" and here his face showed a sudden change, "I shall see her if I am tried for murder. She will be in the court-room,—on the witness stand—"

"Doubtless," I interjected; but his interruption came quickly and with vehement passion.

"Then I am ready. Welcome trial, conviction, death, even. To confront her eye to eye is all I wish. She shall never forget it, never!"

"Then you do not deny——" I began.

"I deny nothing," he returned, and held out his hands with a grim gesture. "How can I, when there falls from everything I touch, the devilish thing which took away the life I hated?"

"Have you anything more to say or do before you leave these rooms?" I asked.

He shook his head, and then, bethinking himself, pointed to the roll of paper which he had flung on the table.

"Burn that!" he cried.

I took up the roll and looked at it. It was the manuscript of a poem in blank verse.

"I have been with it into a dozen newspaper and magazine offices," he explained with great bitterness. "Had I succeeded in getting a publisher for it I might have forgotten my wrongs and tried to build up a new life on the ruins of the old. But they would not have it, none of them, so I say, burn it! that no memory of me may remain in this miserable world."

"Keep to the facts!" I severely retorted. "It was while carrying this poem from one newspaper to another that you secured that bit of print upon the blank side of which you yourself printed the obituary notice with which you savored your revenge upon the woman who had disappointed you."

"You know that? Then you know where I got the poison with which I tipped the silly toy with which that weak man fooled away his life?"

"No," said I, "I do not know where you got it. I merely know it was no common poison bought at a druggist's, or from any ordinary chemist."

"It was woorali; the deadly, secret woorali. I got it from—but that is another man's secret. You will never hear from me anything that will compromise a friend. I got it, that is all. One drop, but it killed my man."

The satisfaction, the delight, which he threw into these words are beyond description. As they left his lips a jet of flame from the neglected fire shot up and threw his figure for one instant into bold relief upon the lowering ceiling; then it died out, and nothing but the twilight dusk remained in the room and on the countenance of this doomed and despairing man.